TABLE OF CONTENTS

CHAPTER 1

MUSIC MOUNTAIN

CAMP
LA LA LAKE
Okay campers, let's make some **noise** out there!

WOOT-WOOT! YEAHHHH!!! WOO-HOOOOO!

Tell us what's up, **Meg!**
You got it!

We're down to the last two teams for today's **Big Bunk Battle** event. . . .
. . . It's **Bunk M** up against **Bunk J** in the final round of the **tug-of-war!**

We've got this!
You ready, **Trey?**
I think so.
Zook?
I'm the strongest kazoo in the world!!!
Love it. **Cordy?**
All set, **Kaylee!**

Ha! No **way** we're losing to **Junk Bunk!**
You guys are a **joke.**

First team to pull the flag to their side **wins!**
Ready . . . **GO!**

SNAP

>MMPH!<
Pull harder!
You pull harder!

Don't let up, team—we can do this!

>HRRMPH!<
Time to go
BEAST MODE!

GRAAAAAHHHH!!!
Dude . . . seriously?

>HRRMPH!<
>GRRMMPH!<

Now's our chance!
One, two, three . . .
HEAVE-HO!

Uh-oh . . .
SLIP

. . . OH NO!

Can't . . .

. . . stop . . .

. . . STRETCHING!

WAAAAAAAH!!!
We have a **winner!**

WHAM

Congratulations, **BUNK M!**
With this victory, Bunk M takes the **top spot** in the competition, while Bunk J drops down to **third place.**

Top of the charts—just where we should be.
HAHAHAHAHAHAHAHA!!!
Better luck **next time,** losers!

Maybe you should just **give up.**
HA! Yeah, that was **brutal** to watch.

Last I checked, **Bunk R** was in . . .
. . . what was it again?
Oh yeah— **last** place!
FLOP

Your **beast** mode is more like **least** mode.
FLEX
FLEX
FLEX

Sorry, I couldn't hear you over the sound of my **intense power posing.**

Ooh! Those Junk Bunk kids are **really** getting on my nerves.
I hate to say it, but they're gonna be **tough** to beat.

If only there was some way to break them up . . .
Now you're talking!
We've just gotta be ready to **strike**. . . .

Sometimes I forget how **ripped** I am.
I'm really sorry about slipping back there . . .

. . . and for screwing up in the last few challenges too.
In fact, we'd probably be **winning** if it wasn't for me.

Ho-ho!
Good show, Bunk J. **Good show!**

It has been an absolute **pleasure** watching you develop into such a **strong team** in this year's Big Bunk Battle.

I guess you haven't been watching **me**, specifically, Dr. Glockenspiel.
I **stink**!
Ho-ho! There's no **"I"** in **"team."**

Win or lose—just have **fun** doing it together. **That's** what matters!

Cordy is taking these losses pretty hard, you guys.
We should try to cheer her up!

I've got it!
We should throw her a super-special-super-**secret**-super-duper **surprise party!**

OH BOY, A SURPRISE PARTY FOR CORDY!!!

Did you say something, Zook?
Gah!
Yeah! Wait'll you hear about—

I could've sworn I just heard my name.
What are you all talking about?
>mmmmph!<

Uh, **COMIC BOOKS!**
And **SOFT TACOS!**

>Phew!<
That was a close one, but I don't think she suspects a thing!

I **knew** it . . .
. . . they blame me **too!**

CHAPTER 2

Pssst! Zook! Over here . . .

. . . we have to start planning for the surprise party!

I'm thinking we should **split up** to cover more ground.
Good idea!

Hold it . . .
. . . we probably look **really** suspicious. . . .

Hi.
GAH!!!

What are you talking about now?

CRUNCHY TACOS!
DEFINITELY NOTHING SECRET!
COMIC BOOKS AGAIN!

Hmmm . . .

Heads up, campers—announcement incoming!
Tomorrow's Big Bunk Battle challenge will be . . .

. . . a **team hike** to the top of **Piccolo Peak!**
First bunk to successfully retrieve the flag at the top **wins.**

Wow! A group hike sounds like a blast!
Good luck, Bunk J!!
Sounds like it could be **tough**.

I studied **maps** of the **whole mountain** before I even got here.

I think I could actually be a ***huge*** help for this challenge tomorrow!

Tomorrow?!?
That's the same day as the **SUR-**

The **SURFING LESSONS!**
Down at the **lake!**
Shhh!
>mmmph!<

But . . . there's no **waves** at the lake. . . .

That's why we need lessons!
Anyhoo, we should give you some **quiet time** to learn more about the mountain!
But I—

Yessir, a quality **solo study session** is **just** what you need.
Right, Trey?
It is?

Oh! I mean, **it is!**
I **totally** agree.

But—
No **buts!**
You stay **right here** and hit the books—we'll get going.
Bye now!

We need to gather all of the stuff for the party **without** Cordy finding out.

How're we gonna pull that off when we all **live** together?

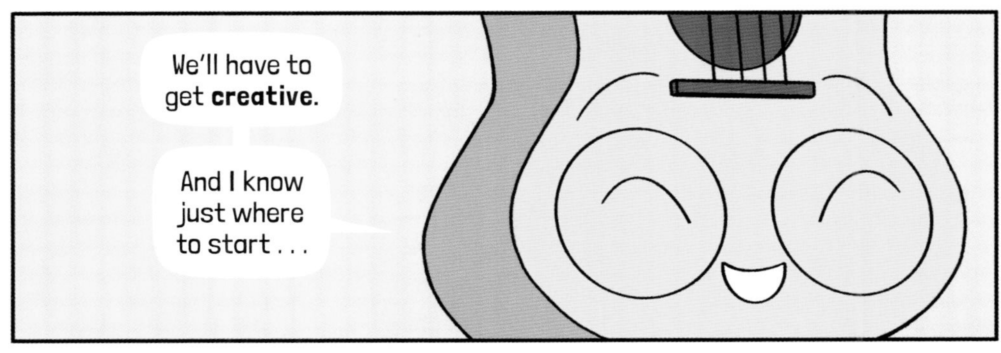
We'll have to get **creative**.
And I know just where to start . . .

. . . the **ARTS and CRAFTS CABIN!**

Excellent work, campers!
Express yourselves—don't worry about making a mess!

That's a **lovely** bracelet!
Did you know that **papier mâché** means ***chewed paper*** in French?
Gross!

Finally, the last piece. **All done!**

CHIRP
CHIRP
CHIRP

Hmmm.
? ? ?

SCRIBBLE
SCRIBBLE

HMMMPH!

Hmm?

An **F**?
I failed?!?
F

How do you **fail** at **popsicle stick birdhouse making?**
The birds are **quite picky** when it comes to **home inspection**, my dear.

Hi! Are you **Ms. Paulette?**

Camp Lala Lake's **master crafter** and **artist extraordinaire?**
The one and only!

My, my, my—such **vibrant colors!**
What brings you three to my incredible **cabin** of **creativity?**

We're throwing a **surprise party** for our friend and want to make some **decorations** for our bunk!

Wonderful!
I suggest making a **celebration sign** out of paper letters, and perhaps some **festive stars?**

I can do that!

Awesome, Trey!
Do you know where I can find some **balloons,** Ms. P?

Hmm . . . I seem to recall some balloons and a helium tank left over from last year's end of summer celebration.
Check the **counselors' cabin!**

Will do!
We should totally get a **cake** from the mess hall too.

OOH! OOH!
Let me do that one. I'm **STARVING!**

Uh . . .
It's not for eating **now**.
The cake is for the **surprise party** tomorrow.

Think about it—what **BIGGER** surprise could there be if I eat it ***before*** the party?

>SIGH<
Promise me you will **not** eat the cake.
Okay, **fine.**
We'll do it ***your*** way.
But seriously, **how** are we gonna sneak all of this stuff back into our bunk if Cordy is there doing her research?
Ah-**hah!** Leave that part up to me! I have a plan.

All right!
Now that everyone has their assignment, let's bring it in.

This is gonna make Cordy **so** happy!
YES! Let's **do** this!
Ready? On three!
One, two, three . . .

. . . OPERATION SURPRISE PARTY!

Meet back at the bunk when you're done!
Good luck!

CHAPTER 3

Whoa! No way . . .

"Music Mountain has long been considered a hot spot of BIGFOOT ACTIVITY."

I KNEW IT!
I wonder if I'll ever actually see one!

CORDY!
GAH!

That's how we're gonna win the team hike—with **outside-the-box** thinking!

Everyone thinks we're gonna **ZIG**, and then we **ZAG!**

Yessir, nothing like a good old **field expedition!**
Have fun out there—gotta go—bye!

And be sure to stay out there for **at least** an hour—er, make that **two** hours!

There is **definitely** something weird going on.
It's like **my only friends** are **avoiding me!**

Stay **positive**, Cordy.
If I can prove myself in the next challenge, then **everything** will go back to normal.

Let's see, where was I . . .
"Despite their reclusive nature, it is common knowledge that bigfoots will often gather to play **volleyball**."

Huh! Probably because they're so **tall**.

"Bigfoots are also excellent at **hiding**, often using the mountain's **natural terrain** as a disguise."

Amazing!

AHHHHH–

–CHOO!

Bless you!

Wow!
I never thought I'd find a rare **Sneezing Sycamore** all the way up here!

Focus, Cordy.
You've got to get a plan together for the group hike!
Speaking of which . . .

. . . I wonder what everybody else is doing?
>HUFF!< >HUFF!< >HUFF!<
I hope the coast is clear.

Perfecto!

This party is gonna **rock**!

Trey! How'd you do with the decorations?
It was a lot of fun!

Is that you, Kaylee?
Great! I've got the balloons—

Oh no! **She's back! Quick**—hide these!!!
WHERE?!?

No—**WAIT**!!!

What now?
Am I supposed to come in through **the window**?
It's not what it looks like!

What are you talking about?
Looks like our **regular old bunk** to me.

Wha—?
How?!?
I know you said two hours, but I needed a different book.
Uh-huh . . .

What have you been up to?
Yep!

Are you even **listening** to me?
Sounds good!

Whatever.
I'll get on that right away!

>pssst!<
Trey! Where are you?!?

I'm up here!
HELP!!!

That was some **quick thinking**!
BOING

I had **nothing** to do with it!
If we were outside, I would've floated into **outer space**!

GRAB
Ha! You'd be the first **AS-*TREY*-NAUT**!

Touch-down!
Now let's hide these before Cordy comes back!

Cordy?
If you're in
there, close
your eyes!
You're all
good, Zook.

Check it out!
Ooh!
Wow!

Great job, Zook!

Wait a sec . . .
What
happened
THERE?

Uh . . . looks **fine** to me.
Let's see those **hands.**
BOTH of them!

We told you **not** to eat the cake!
I **didn't!**
I was **about** to.

Oh no!
Cordy's coming back!

Everybody, act normal! Zook, do something about that **cake blob!**

With **pleasure!**

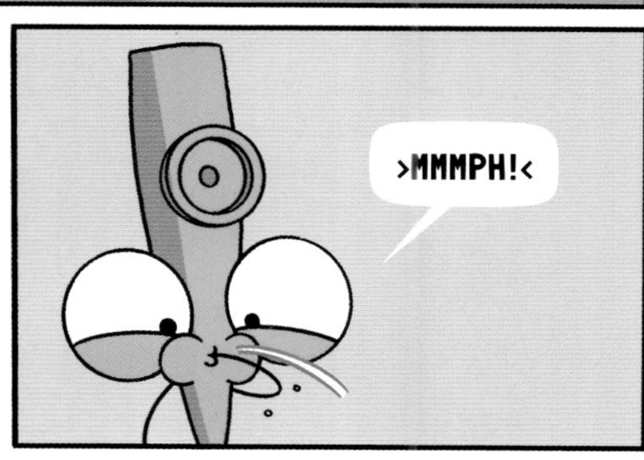
>MMMPH!<

I grabbed the wrong book—
Oh! Hey everyone!

I'm making some good progress with the game plan for tomorrow.
>mmhmm!<

Um . . . does **anyone** wanna do research with me?

Uh—I'd love to! But . . . I have to . . . **iron** my . . . **socks!**
That's **right!** And I have to **help!**
>mmhmm!<

Okay.
Guess I'll get going.

Not that anyone cares. . . .

>PHEW!<
Keeping this secret is **tough!**
She seems ***really*** down in the dumps.

That's why we need to make this the **greatest** surprise party **ever!**

It's worse than I thought!

They **are** mad at me. . . .

. . . Kaylee doesn't even **own** socks!
HOP

Sounds like **trouble** in Junk Bunk to me.
Hee-hee! Music to my ears . . .
Just follow my lead . . .

You'll never believe what I heard about **JUNK BUNK!**

Yeah, ***everybody's*** talking about their one **weak link**.
What?!? Other kids are talking about Junk Bunk?

Only the **whole camp!**

What are they saying?!?

All I know is that **one** of the Junk Bunk team members is letting their team down.
BIG time.
I heard they might even get **kicked out!**

I'd **hate** to be them!
They **must** be talking about me!

This is **terrible**. . . . I don't wanna get kicked out!

I've got to do something, and **FAST.**

CHAPTER 4
THE NEXT MORNING . . .
Rise and shine, campers. . . .

. . . Let's hope the **sun** decides to do the same in time for today's challenge!

>YAWN!<
Huh?

Kaylee! Zook!
Look—Cordy is already up and gone!

She's probably **already** at the mess hall waiting for the challenge to start.

This is the **perfect** opportunity to **decorate.**

If we get everything ready **now**, we can surprise Cordy after our **big win!**

Let's get to it!
YEAH!!!

LATER . . .
Great work everybody—the bunk looks **amazing!**
Wish I could say the same about this weather. . . .
MESS HALL

Remember, Zook, **don't** mention the party.
Who, **me?** Of course not!
Riiiiiight . . .

Speaking of Cordy, do either of you see her?
Nope!
Not yet.

She must be here somewhere.
Let's split up and search!
May I have your attention, please!

Due to the **inclement weather**, today's challenge will be **postponed.**
Aww **maaaan!**
Bummer!

I know, I know . . .
. . . all campers shall **remain** in the mess hall to wait out the storm.

Did you find her?
No luck!
Cordy is **definitely** missing.

Ha! Looks like you're short one **loser!**
I *wonder* **what** could have happened to them?

Oooh!
Of **course** your bunk is involved somehow.
Where's Cordy?

I saw her heading towards Piccolo Peak this morning—on her **own**!

Junk Bunk is **soooo** gonna be **disqualified** from this challenge!

HAHAHAHAHAHA!!!
That ***can't*** be true.
Why would she tackle the team hike **all by herself?**

Not only **that**, but it's **dangerous** out there. . . .
. . . We should tell **Meg!**

We can't **tattle** on our own teammate—she'll get in **big** trouble!

Zook's right, we've gotta fix this as a team.
But Meg said to **stay** in the mess hall!

That's why we have to be ***sneaky***. . . .
Ready?

Go!
Yikes! It's raining **even harder** out here now!

I sure hope Cordy's okay. . . .
Ugh. Can't let this weather stop me.
If I prove I can win this all by myself . . .
. . . there's **no way** they'll want to kick me out!

A **cave!**
Getting out of the rain for a bit would be **nice**, but I have to keep moving.

Besides, there're probably **bigfoots** in there anyway.

Hrrm?

There's no sign of this rain letting up anytime soon.
Thank goodness we're all **safe inside.**
MESS HALL

Wait a sec . . .
. . . where's **Bunk J?**

Say, have any of the Bunk J crew grabbed lunch yet?

Hmm . . . now that you mention it, I haven't seen **any** of them.
Normally that **Zook** kid has had **several helpings** by now.
I don't know **where** he **puts** it all!

>SNICKER!<
Junk Bunk is so busted!
>Pfft!<

Ah, Bunk R—acting more suspicious than usual, I see.
You wouldn't know anything about Bunk J's whereabouts, would you?

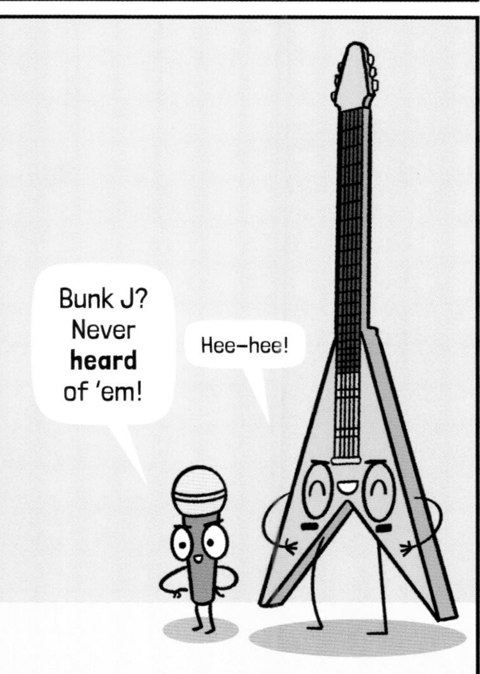
Bunk J? Never heard of 'em!
Hee-hee!

Riiiiight.
Let's try that again. . . .

Okay! According to the map there are **several routes** to Piccolo Peak.
Which way do you think Cordy went?

One thing is for sure . . .
. . . we should avoid the **Falsetto Falls** route entirely.

Why's that?
It's the most dangerous trail.
It would be **IMPOSSIBLE** on a day like today!

Thankfully, Cordy's **way too smart** to even attempt it.

Oh boy—the **Rhythm River!**

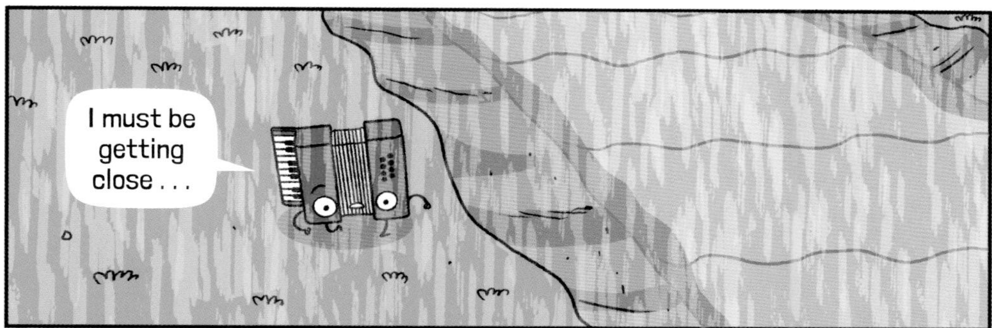
I must be getting close . . .

>GULP!<

It's a **lot bigger** in person.

Falsetto Falls. Maybe this wasn't such a great idea. . . .

Confidence, Cordy! Just one easy climb up and the flag is all yours.

>HUP!<
>HUP!<
>HUP!<

That wasn't so tough. . . .

. . . Onward and upward!

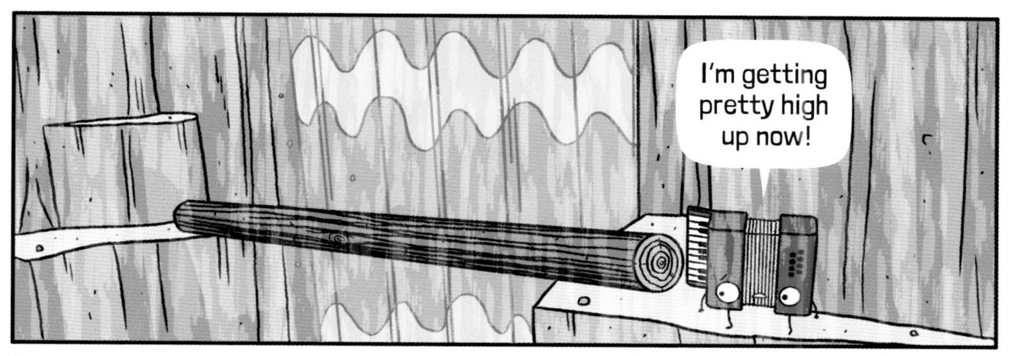
I'm getting pretty high up now!

Don't look down, don't look down, don't look down . . .

GAH!
I just said ***don't*** look down!

Yes—made it!
What's **next?**

>HUP!<
>HUP!<
>HUP!<

This part looks **tricky** . . .

. . . maybe not!

You are **crushing** this, Cor—
SLIP

—deeEE—YEE YIKES!

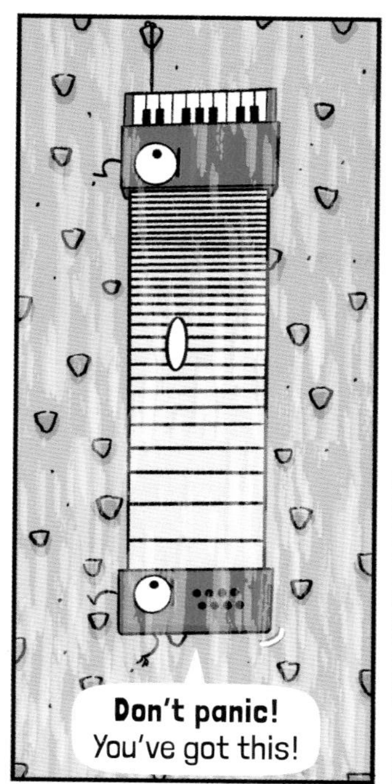
Don't panic! You've got this!

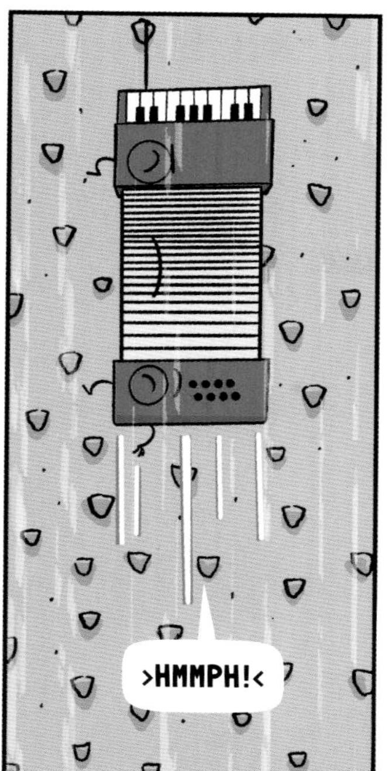
>HMMPH!<

Slow and **steady** does it.

Phew! Thank goodness the rain stopped!

That was a close one . . .
. . . but it looks like **smooth sailing** from here!
KRAK
AAAAAAAHHH!!!

CHAPTER 5

MEANWHILE . . .
C'mon team—we're **almost there!**

We did it!
We made it to **Piccolo Peak!**

WOOT-WOOT!
But—if the flag is still here . . .

. . . where's **Cordy?!?**
HELLLLLLPPP!!!

CORDY!!!

HEY! I'm stuck down here!!!

Oh man!!! What're we gonna do?!?
I'M TOTALLY FREAKING OUT!

Don't freak out!
I think I have a plan!

Hold on, Cordy— we're coming!

How did you know where to find me?

I'll explain later!
For now . . .

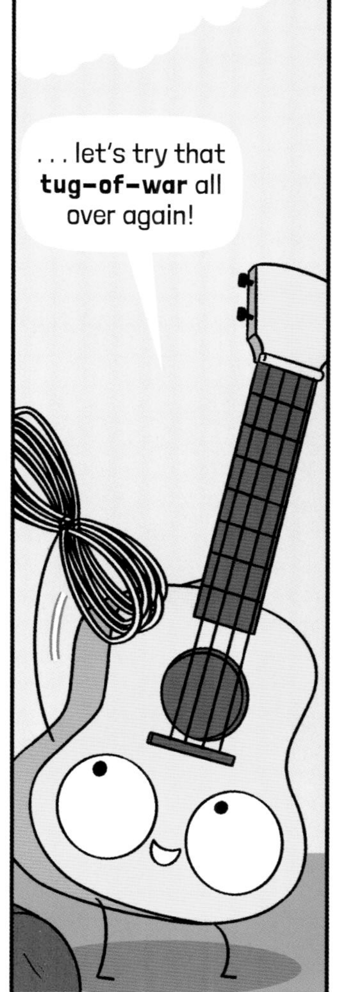
. . . let's try that tug-of-war all over again!

Everyone ready?
BEAST MODE initiated!

Get ready to grab on, Cordy!
Okay!

Now try to **stretch** as we **pull!**

HEAVE!

HO!!!

YES!!!
We're **halfway there!**

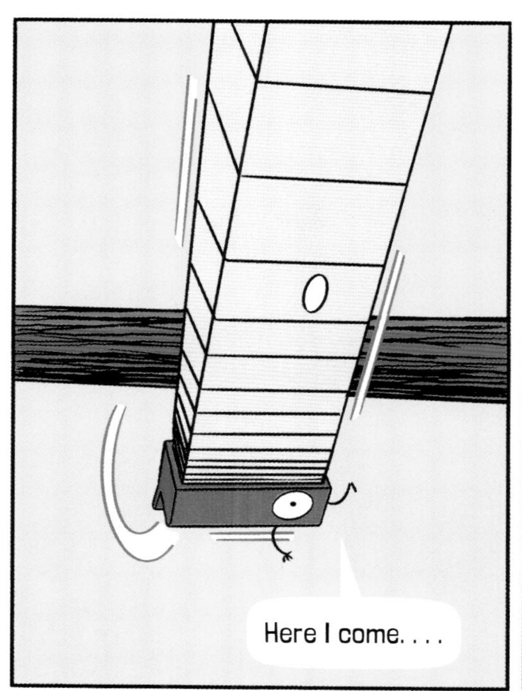
Here I come. . . .

WE DID IT!
You saved me!

You're not ditching **this** team so easily.
That's **right**!

Now let's **beat** this challenge **together!**

Well, well, **well** . . .

. . . **look** what we have **here.**

You kids have **a lot** of **explaining** to do.

A SHORT TIME LATER . . .
. . . and that's how we all wound up at Piccolo Peak.
So—I guess all's well that ends well, right?
HA! No.
You're disqualified from this round, but you displayed some A+ teamwork.

So . . . great job, but don't ever sneak out again.
Understood?

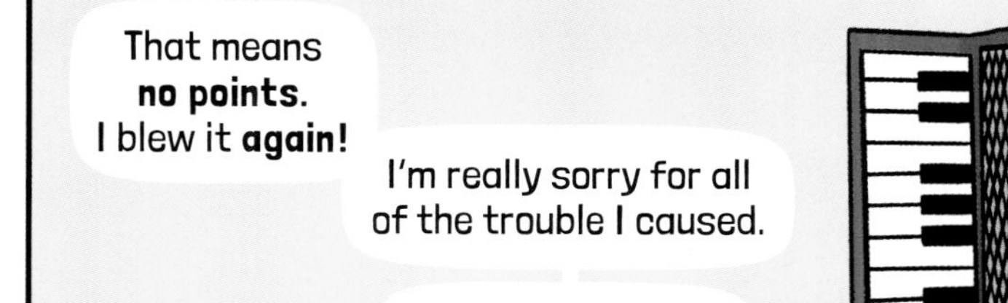
That means no points. I blew it again!
I'm really sorry for all of the trouble I caused.
I get it if you wanna kick me out.

Whaaa-?!?
Why would we ever do that?

Ha! It's more like the **complete opposite**. . . .

S RP ISE
CORDY
J
SURPRISE TO OUR BEST FRIEND CORDY!!!
>GASP!<
All this, for **me**?

We think you're the **best** no matter what.
YASSSSS!!!

Now let's **celebrate** with some **cake!**

Uhh . . .
. . . I can **explain.**
ZOOK!!!

Brian "Smitty" Smith is a former Marvel Comics and DC Comics editor. He is the creator and writer behind the Officer Clawsome series of books, as well as the creator of the Pea, Bee, & Jay graphic novels. Smitty lives in Greensboro, North Carolina.